W9-BXF-718

Memories I Keep In My Heart

BY GAIL A. ORANGE M.S.L.S.

Peace Power
& Many Blessings
Gail Orange
MSLS

Memories I Keep In My Heart © 2012 by My Vision Works Publishing
Farmington Hills, MI 48334

Contributors:
Book Interior and Cover Design-My Vision Works Publishing
Illustrations-Ryan A. Gering
Editor-in-Chief-Rhonda Boggess
Publishing Assistant-Jana` White

All rights reserved. No part of this book may be reproduced or transmitted in any form or by any means, electronic or mechanical, including information storage and retrieval systems, without permission in writing from the publisher.

Printed in the United States of America.

ISBN-13: 978-1477401323
ISBN-10: 1477401326

Library of Congress Cataloging-in-Publication Data

Memories I Keep in My Heart: Gail Orange

1. Children
2. Storybook
3. Inspirational

For marketing and publicity, please contact:

My Vision Works Publishing
www.myvisionworkspublishing.com
myvisionworkspublishing@gmail.com
248-254-3847

This dedication is to all of my grandchildren because electronic toys have replaced mud pies.

This story is a part of your history. You need to know that God answers prayer if it is in line with His will. God is not a bully. His will is for our highest good.

Love Always and Forever,

Grandmommie

Matthew 6:10: "Thy will be done on earth as it is in heaven."

I would like to thank God, Colin Carmichael, Katherine Frisby-Owens, Lois Carmichael-Drafts, Shirley Bogins, Francis Hayden and the Nelson family for the memories that I keep in my heart.

~Gail A. Nelson-Orange, MSLS Urban Librarian

Author's Notes

I feel that it is important for children to understand their roots. Today there are so many things to grab and hold their attention. If they are to be successful in life they need a strong foundation. It is for this purpose that I have written this book. I am hopeful that the many teachers and parents that need this type of faith-based picture book will enjoy reading and discussing it.

I remember walking to school with Colin.

How do you get to school?

Who brings you to school?

I remember piano lessons with Katherine.

Do you know anyone who plays a musical instrument?

What musical instrument would you like to learn to play?

I **remember** watching Lois weave on a loom. She is making cloth for a dress.

Have you ever made anything to wear?

What would you like to learn to make?

I remember making mud pies in the back yard with Shirley.

What games do you play outdoors?

Who do you like to play with outdoors?

I **remember** praying with my family for a larger place to live. We believed that the family that prayed together, stayed together.

Does your family pray together?

Do you have a favorite prayer?

I **remember** moving to a larger place and understanding that God answers prayer.

"Be anxious for nothing, but in everything by prayer and supplication, with thanksgiving, let your requests be made known to God;"-- Philippians 4:6

"Now faith is the substance of things hoped for, the evidence of things not seen."-- Hebrews 11:1

I **remember** playing baseball in the street.

Do you know how to play baseball?

Have you ever been to a baseball game?

I remember walking to the public library with my class.

Have you ever made a visit to the public library?

Do you have a library card?

I **remember** writing letters to my cousin
Francis in secret code.

Do you have a friend or relative that lives far away?

How do you let them know what a great life you are living?

And, best of all **I remember** riding, riding, riding my bike to visit my friends Pat and Flora.

Do you have new friends?

Will you keep your **old friends**?

What memories do you keep
in your heart?

14929682R00014

Made in the USA
Charleston, SC
08 October 2012